The
Twin Giants

The Twin Giants

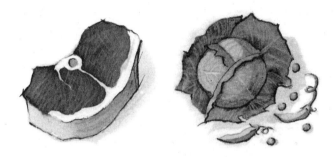

DICK KING-SMITH

illustrated by **Mini Grey**

WALKER BOOKS

First published 2007 by Walker Books Ltd
87 Vauxhall Walk, London SE11 5HJ

This edition published 2013

2 4 6 8 10 9 7 5 3 1

Text © 2007 Foxbusters Ltd
Illustrations © 2007 Mini Grey

The right of Dick King-Smith and Mini Grey to be identified as
author and illustrator respectively of this work has been asserted by them
in accordance with the Copyright, Designs and Patents Act 1988

This book has been typeset in Adobe Caslon

Printed and bound in Italy by ▲ Grafica Veneta S.p.A.

British Library Cataloguing in Publication Data:
a catalogue record for this book is available from the British Library

ISBN 978-1-4063-5337-2

www.walker.co.uk

For Mavis

M. G.

Mountain Number 1

The Seven Mountains

Mountain
Number One

ONCE UPON A MOUNTAIN, THERE lived two brother giants. Twin brothers, in fact, something that's rare among giants. When the first one was born, his giant father looked at the huge baby and said …

And when the second one arrived,
his giant mother looked at the huge
baby and said ...

"There's a-lot-ov-'im!"

Time passed and Lottavim and Normus

grew … and grew.

They loved playing games. They
liked races –

Down the Mountain

(start from the top, first to reach the bottom wins)

and

Up the Mountain

(start from the bottom, first to reach the top wins).

The finish of these races was always close, often a dead heat, and the time they took for each race grew shorter as the giants' legs grew longer.

And they liked to play a game called Roll the Boulder. They would choose two gigantic lumps of rock and put them side by side at the top of the mountain. Then one or other (they took turns) would shout "Roll!" and each would give his rock a shove, and down the mountainside

the two great lumps would go bouncing. The winner was the one whose boulder went the furthest.

The other thing that Lottavim and Normus liked to do was sing. They would sit side by side outside the cave where they lived, and sing the songs their giant parents had taught them, very very loudly of course. This might not have been too bad if either of them had been able to sing in tune, but neither could, and in the rich and fertile valley below the mountain, mothers would tell their naughty children, "Behave yourselves, or the giants will get you."

Lottavim and Normus always did everything together. They walked in step with one another. They woke up and went to sleep at exactly the same time. They even sneezed at the same moment.

AAAHcHOO

But the twins
were different
in one way…

Lottavim liked meat.

Normus liked vegetables.

This had been the case right from the start. When their parents raided the farms and market gardens in the rich and fertile valley below, they might bring back, say, a nice spring lamb and a couple of dozen young cabbages, and Lottavim would always make a grab for the lamb and Normus would always lunge for the cabbages.

Now giants do not live very long lives, and when

18

the twins were only twelve years old and twelve feet high, both their parents died.

So Lottavim and Normus had to learn to find their own food. Twice a week, on Wednesdays and Saturdays, they would thunder down the mountainside, each with a great sack slung over his shoulder, and make the rounds of farms and market gardens, and of dairies and henhouses and beehives and orchards (for Lottavim *did* like fruit and Normus was *rather* fond of milk and eggs and honey).

On those days the people of
the rich and fertile valley locked
themselves in their houses, all
hoping the giants would steal
someone else's
produce.

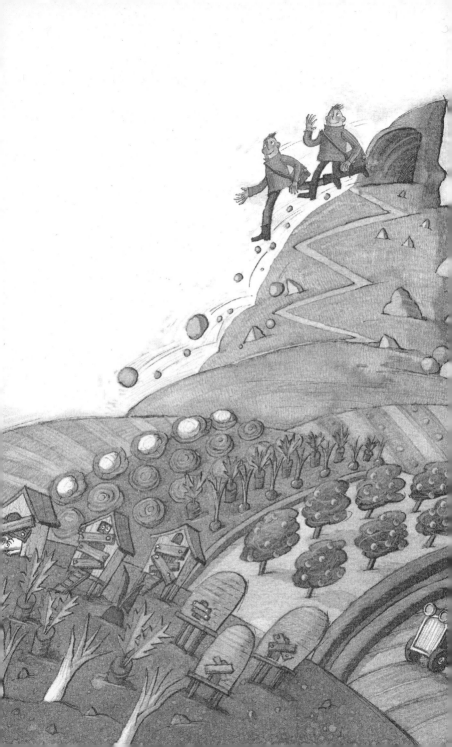

They had to learn how to cook too, and how to keep a tidy cave. After a time they got used to it – though each always said to the other, "The one person I couldn't do without is you, Lottavim," or "you, Normus," depending which one was speaking.

Only when they reached the age of twenty and the height of eighteen feet did Lottavim and Normus stop growing. To look at, if anyone had been brave enough to take a good close look at them (which no one was), they were almost impossible to tell apart. They still did everything

at the same time, but now that
they were grown-up, something
changed, for both of them.

For a time they did not discuss
this change openly, but one evening
after supper, when Lottavim had
just polished off a baron of beef and
Normus was chock-full of chickpeas
and cheese and chives, they looked
at one another and each knew,
beyond the shadow of a doubt, just
what his brother was thinking.

With one breath they said,
"It's about time I found a
wife," and the very next
morning, off they set.

Mountain Number Two & Mountain Number Three

THERE WERE OF COURSE PLENTY of girls of marriageable age in the rich and fertile valley below, but neither twin was in the least interested in such midgets, mostly less than five and a half feet tall.

No, no, what each had in mind was nothing less than the giantess of his dreams.

Giants and giantesses – the brothers had been taught – lived only in the mountains, up or down which they, with their twelve-foot strides, could walk twice as easily as ordinary folk. So Lottavim and Normus wasted no time in the valley behind their home but marched across it, side by side and keeping step, and climbed the mountain beyond.

Near its summit, they met a very old, white-haired giant who said, "Hullo. Who are you and what do you want?"

The twins introduced themselves.

"We're each looking for a wife, sir," they said politely. "Do you have any daughters?"

"One," said the old giant. "She's out, getting my lunch."

Just then they heard a rattle of stones further down the mountainside and saw a figure coming up the slope. As the figure drew closer, the twins saw that it was a giantess carrying a dead sheep across her shoulders and almost as tall as they were. With one voice they said to her, "Will you marry me?"

The giantess gave a giant giggle.
"I can't marry both of you!"

"Oh," said Lottavim.

"Oh," said Normus.

"And anyway, I'm afraid I can't marry either of you. I've got to look after my old dad."

"Hard luck, boys!" grinned the old giant.

As they plunged away down the mountainside with giant strides, Normus said, "I've been thinking, Lot."

"So have I, Norm," said Lottavim, "and I've had an idea."

"Me too," said Normus. "If we do meet any other girls, we shall only be competing against one another."

"Exactly. But if we split up for a while, each of us might find what he's looking for on his own."

"Exactly."

So when they reached the next mountain, each went his separate way, Lottavim up one side and Normus up the other.

It was not long before Lottavim came upon a young giantess sitting on a rock, eating raw runner beans. There's no time to waste, he thought, so he said, "Hullo and are you married, and if not will you marry me?"

"You're a fast worker," said the giantess. "The answers are – no, I'm not married, and it depends."

"Depends on what?"

"Whether you eat meat."

"Of course I do," said Lottavim.

"In that case," said the giantess, "I'm afraid I wouldn't marry you if you were the last giant on earth. I strongly disapprove of meat-eating.

I'm a vegetarian."

Wow! thought Lottavim, just right for my brother. And he hurried away, shouting, "Norm! Norm! Where are you?"

Normus, round the other side of the mountain, had also come across a young giantess, who was also sitting on a rock, gnawing a beef bone.

"Hullo," he said. "I'm looking for a single girl, with a view to marriage. Any chance you're free?"

"You don't mess about, do you?" she replied. "Yes, I'm free. Have a bit of my bone."

"No thanks," said Normus. "I'm a vegetarian."

"Oh dear, oh dear," said the giantess. "The giant I marry has to like meat."

Wow! thought Normus, just right for my brother. And he hurried away, shouting, "Lot! Lot! Where are you?"

When the brothers had met and told one another what had happened, each set off round the mountain to meet the giantess the other had found. Each now knew that the giantesses were single, so when Lottavim found the beef-eater, he pitched straight in.

"Will you marry me?" he said.

"I've already said no," she replied.

"That was my twin brother," said Lottavim. "I'm a meat-eater."

"Twin brother!" she said.
"Ha ha, funny joke."

When Normus came upon
the bean-eating giantess, he too
wasted no words, but immediately
proposed.

"I've already refused you,"
she said.

"That was my twin brother,"
said Normus. "I'm a vegetarian."

"Twin brother!" she said. "Pull
the other one."

When the brothers met again, Lottavim said, "I told her I was a meat-eater, Norm, but she said no."

"I told her I was a vegetarian, Lot," said Normus, "but she said no."

"Talk about fussy," said Lottavim. "Why can't they be easy-going like us?"

"Exactly," said Normus. "Why can't a giantess be more like a giant?" And side by side and keeping step, they marched away towards the next mountain.

Mountains Number Four, Five & Six

BUT THOUGH THEY CLIMBED IT
and searched thoroughly, they found
no one. Nor did they on the fifth
mountain. Nor on the sixth.

For old times' sake, they ran some races and played a few games of Roll the Boulder, but they met no giantesses. Normus got downhearted. "Let's go back home, Lot," he said. "We're never going to find wives."

Lottavim put his huge arm round his brother's huge shoulders. "Oh, come on now, Norm," he said. "The next mountain will be the seventh, and seven's a lucky number."

Mountain Number Seven

"FINGERS CROSSED, NORM," SAID Lottavim as they reached the foot of the seventh mountain, and each of them crossed two of their ten-inch fingers. Then they went their separate ways up the steep slopes.

On the eastern side of the mountain Normus came upon a family of giants. They made him very welcome, offering him a whole sucking-pig, which of course he refused, pretending that he had just eaten, but in fact, quite hungry by now, he accepted a small snack of a dozen apples, six pears and a pumpkin.

There was a mother giant and a father giant and three giant children, all boys.

"Fine sons you have," said
Normus to the father when he
could get a word in, for they were a
talkative lot. "No daughters?"

"No," said the mother.

"You married?" asked the father.

"No," said Normus.

Father and mother looked at
one another and smiled.

"Try the other side of
the mountain,"
they said.

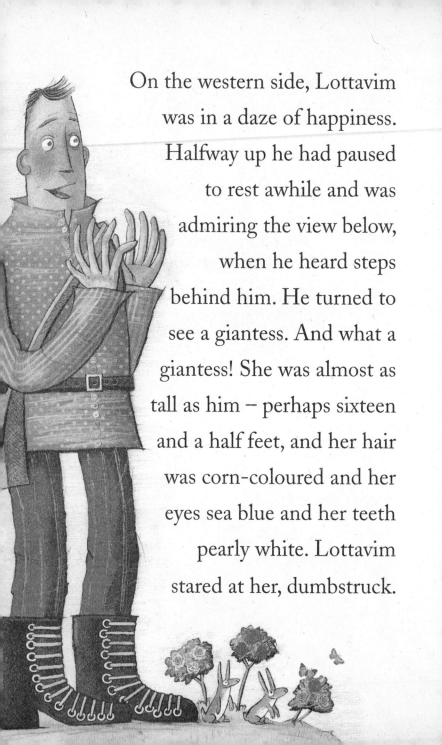

On the western side, Lottavim was in a daze of happiness. Halfway up he had paused to rest awhile and was admiring the view below, when he heard steps behind him. He turned to see a giantess. And what a giantess! She was almost as tall as him – perhaps sixteen and a half feet, and her hair was corn-coloured and her eyes sea blue and her teeth pearly white. Lottavim stared at her, dumbstruck.

"Hullo," she said in a voice like warm treacle. "Who are you?"

Lottavim smiled. "My name is Lottavim," he replied.

"My name," said the beautiful giantess, "is Georgina, but you can call me Georgie if you like. Can I do anything for you?"

Oh yes, thought Lottavim, you can be my wife! This is it! This is the real thing! This is love at first sight!

"Tell me you're not married," he said.

"I'm not," said Georgina.

"Tell me you're not a vegetarian."

"I love all sorts of food."

Lottavim took a deep breath. "D'you think," he asked, "that you could love me?"

Georgina burst out laughing. It was a jolly, bubbly laugh, an infectious laugh, and Lottavim found himself laughing with her.

"I like you," she said.

They stared at one another, and then Lottavim reached out and took her huge hand in his even huger one.

"Georgie," he said.

"Yes, Lottavim?"

"I am looking for a wife."

"Look no further."

"Oh Georgie!" said Lottavim. "You've made me the happiest giant in the world!"

Just then they heard a voice calling, "Lot! Lot! Where are you?"

"Who's that?" asked Georgina.

"My twin brother Normus."

"Your twin brother?"

"Yes."

"Identical?"

"Yes," said Lottavim. "He's looking for a wife too," and then, as Normus came into sight, "but it doesn't look as though he's had any luck."

"Norm, old boy," he said when his brother reached them, "allow me to introduce Georgina, Georgie for short."

This is it! thought Normus. This is the real thing! This is love at first sight!

"I hope you'll be very happy, Norm..." said Lottavim – We shall! We shall! thought Normus – "...to know that Georgie and I are going to be married."

Normus's jaw dropped.

He stared at the pair of them, speechless. Then, somehow, he managed a smile. Somehow he stammered out words of congratulation. He stood and watched as the happy couple descended the slopes and set off, hand in hand, for home.

For a long time Normus sat there, the picture of misery. If only I had gone round the western side and Lot round the eastern, he thought. Or if only I hadn't spent so much time eating and talking with that family, I still might have met her first. As it is, Lot is to marry the giantess of my dreams. I shall never meet another like her. And what's more, I shall never see my twin brother again – I couldn't bear to go home and play gooseberry. Two's company, three's none. I'm on my own from now on.

He put his giant head in his giant hands and heaved a giant sigh.

"You don't sound very happy,"
said a voice suddenly, a voice like
warm treacle.

Normus raised his head from his
hands to see Georgina standing before
him, showing her pearly white teeth
in a smile, her sea-blue eyes twinkling,
her corn-coloured hair blowing in the
mountain breeze.

She's come back!
he thought. She's
decided against poor
old Lot. She's chosen
me instead!

"Oh," he said. "So you're not going to marry Lottavim?"

The giantess looked puzzled.

"Marry who?" she asked.

"Lottavim."

"Certainly not."

Normus swallowed.

"I have to tell you," he said, "that I'm a vegetarian."

"Doesn't worry me."

Normus took a deep breath.

"In that case," he said, "will you marry *me*?"

"I quite like that idea," said the beautiful giantess, "though I haven't a clue who you are."

"I'm Lottavim's brother, Normus. Don't you remember me, Georgie?"

"No," said the giantess, "because I'm not Georgie. I'm Alexandra, though you can call me Alex."

"I don't understand," said Normus. "How can you be so *exactly* like Georgie?"

"Because," replied Alexandra, "she is my identical twin sister."

Choose a Mountain

EVEN THOUGH BOTH WERE SO
madly in love – Lottavim with
Georgie, Normus with Alex –
the twin brothers were thinking,
at exactly the same moment,
about each other.

Poor old Norm, thought Lottavim, he'll be so lonely and miserable on his own.

Good old Lot, thought Normus, he'll be so happy to know that I've been as lucky as him.

So when Lottavim was saying to Georgie, "I must go and find Norm, he'll be so unhappy," she replied, "No need. Just look who's coming." For there, striding hand in hand up the slopes of Mountain Number One, were Normus and Alex.

"How on earth … what … who…" gabbled Lottavim. "She looks exactly like you!"

"She's my twin sister Alexandra," said Georgie, "and she is like me in every way, except that I'm in love with you and she, by the look of things, is in love with your brother. He doesn't seem to me to be at all unhappy."

What a celebration there was when the two couples met at the cave!

All four roared so long and
so loudly in their delight that the
villagers in the rich and fertile
valley below thought that the end
of the world was upon them.

"How happy our father and mother would have been for us," said Lottavim to Normus.

"Would have been?" said Georgie. "You mean…?"

"Yes," said Normus, "they died eight years ago."

"How odd," said the sister giantesses.

"Odd?" said the brother giants.

"Yes, because our parents would have been so happy too."

"Would have been?" said Lottavim. "You mean…?"

"Yes," said Georgie. "They died two years ago. Alex and I have lived alone in our cave ever since."

There was a silence. The twin brothers looked at one another. "One cave on Mountain Number One…" said Normus, and "One cave on Mountain Number Seven…" said Lottavim. "Makes one cave for each couple," said Georgie and Alex with one voice, "who's going where?"

Lottavim took a huge
gold coin from his pocket.

"We'll toss for it, shall we, Norm?"
he said. "Heads – Georgie and I will
stay here and you and Alex go back to
the other cave.

Tails – you and

Alex stay here

and Georgie

and I go back."

"All right,"

replied Normus.

I don't care

which cave

I live in

as long as

my brother

is happy, he thought.

Lottavim balanced the huge coin on his huge thumb. I don't care which cave I live in as long as my brother is happy, he thought.

I hope it's "heads", Georgie thought. I like this cave.

I hope it's "heads", Alex thought. I'd sooner go back home.

"Go on then, Lot," said Normus, so Lottavim flipped the huge coin with his giant thumb and it came down "heads".

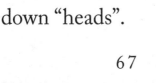

I expect you can guess that, as time went by, there was a great deal of traffic between Mountain Number One and Mountain Number Seven. Life for the villagers in the rich and fertile valley became even more difficult.

At first it was just the two
couples of giants visiting each
other, but later Georgina had
babies and Alexandra had babies

(on the same day, of course).
I say "babies" because (would you
believe it) each of the sisters gave
birth to twins!

On that wonderful day Lottavim charged down from the cave on Mountain Number One, singing at the top of his awful voice, to tell his brother the glad news, and Normus

charged down from the cave on
Mountain Number Seven,
singing at the top of his awful
voice, to tell his brother the
glad news.

"You'll never guess, Norm!" shouted Lottavim as they met, and "You'll never guess, Lot!" shouted Normus, and then they looked at one another and each somehow knew.

"I've got twins," said Normus in what was, for him, a quite quiet voice. "You too?"

"Me too," said Lottavim, and
they gave each other a giant hug.

Also by
Dick King-Smith...

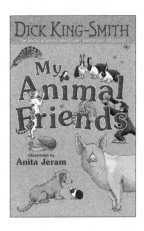

"I thought I would tell you about some of my animal friends."

There's: Dodo the film-star dachshund;
Frank the flop-eared rabbit;
Midnight the angry cow;
Lupin, the cat who thinks he's a dog;
and Nanny Anna, the dog who
plays mum to kittens.

**Wherever Dick King-Smith goes,
unusual animals are sure to follow.**

The Finger-Eater

Ulf, the finger-eating troll, bites off more than he can chew when he meets the plucky Gudrun!

"Amusingly gruesome." *The Daily Telegraph*

"Very, very funny ... the drawings are hilarious."
The Daily Mirror

Dick King-Smith (1922–2011), a former dairy farmer, is one of the world's favourite children's book authors. Winner of the Guardian Children's Fiction Prize for *The Sheep-Pig* (filmed as *Babe*), he was named Children's Book Author of the Year in 1991 and won the 1995 Children's Book Award for *Harriet's Hare*. His titles for Walker include *Aristotle*; *Lady Lollipop* and its sequel, *Clever Lollipop*; *My Animal Friends*; *The Finger-Eater*; and the much-loved Sophie series.

Mini Grey got her name because she was born in a Mini Cooper in a car park. She has written and illustrated several books for children, including *The Adventures of the Dish and the Spoon*, which won the Kate Greenaway Medal, and *Traction Man Is Here*, which was a *New York Times* Best Illustrated Books winner.

Aristotle the kitten is so adventurous that it's
a good thing cats have nine lives. But it's even
better that the kind witch Bella Donna is his
owner. Somehow she is always there to save him.
Is it luck? Or is it a little bit of magic?

"Dick King-Smith is a superb storyteller
and his trademark gentle humour pervades
this tale ... both charming and funny."
The School Librarian